This book belongs to:

_____

_____

_____

First published 1999 by Walker Books Ltd
87 Vauxhall Walk, London SE11 5HJ

8 10 9

Maisy™. Maisy is a registered trademark of Walker Books Ltd, London.

Based on the Audio Visual series "Maisy". A King Rollo Films Production for
PolyGram Visual Programming. Original script by Andrew Brenner.

Lucy Cousins font © 2005 Lucy Cousins

The author/illustrator has asserted her moral rights.

Printed in China

British Library Cataloguing in Publication Data:
a catalogue record for this book is
available from the British Library

ISNBN 978-0-7445-7217-9

www.walker.co.uk

Maisy's Pool

Lucy Cousins

WALKER BOOKS
AND SUBSIDIARIES

LONDON • BOSTON • SYDNEY • AUCKLAND

Maisy and Tallulah
are feeling hot.

Maisy has an idea.
She looks in her
shed ...

and finds the
paddling pool.
Maisy blows it up.
Puff, puff, puff!

Tallulah fills the pool with water.

Maisy and Tallulah put on their swimming costumes. Ready, steady...

Oh dear, the paddling pool has a hole in it!

Maisy mends the hole with sticky tape. That's better.

Then along comes
Eddie in his
swimming trunks ...

and sits in the pool! Oh Eddie, there's no room for Maisy and Tallulah.

But Eddie gives
Maisy and Tallulah
a shower.
Now everyone is cool.

If you're crazy for Maisy, you'll love these other books featuring Maisy and her friends.

Other titles

Maisy's ABC • Maisy Goes to Bed • Maisy Goes to the Playground

Maisy Goes Swimming • Maisy Goes to Playschool

Maisy's House • Happy Birthday, Maisy • Maisy at the Farm